# Introduction

Growing up in a New York City apartment, my pets were limited to parakeets, goldfish and those little turtles you once found at the five and dime store. What I really longed for was a dog. To me, that was a 'real' pet—an animal you could take for a walk, play with, hug and have a friendship with.

After I was married and moved to a home of my own, my dream finally came true. I brought home an eight week old Apricot Poodle and named him Woody. What happened during the next 16 years was a beautiful friendship. I laughed, I learned, I cried, I loved. It completely exceeded my expectations and taught me lessons about life and love that will stay with me forever.

These tales are based on true stories — just some of the antics that have happened since the *Poodle Posse* has grown. It has the cute, little characters, happy endings and good morals that would appeal to young readers, but I suspect it would also put a smile on the faces of all dog lovers.

*Chrysa Smith*

**Posse:** *a group of friends or associates*

~~~~~~~~~~

Dedicated to the memory of my first *angel with paws*

Woody

# The Adventures of the Poodle Posse

by Chrysa Smith

*Illustrated by Pat Achilles*

# The Case of the
# Missing Steak Bone

Mrs. Flout pulled open the kitchen door. She crumbled up some day old bread and sprinkled it across the yard now covered with a thick, hard layer of snow. She always liked to feed the birds, especially in the winter. In fact, she was an animal lover of the highest order. A plump woman who had blown out more birthday candles than she could remember, Francine Flout had rosy cheeks, white hair, wire-rim glasses, an apron and a spoon in her hand. She loved to cook, look at the birds and pamper her two favorite kids — her apricot and black miniature poodles.

With no real children of her own, Francine Flout put all her love and time into her little posse, as she called them. There was Archie; a jumpy little guy with a pile of black curls. He was kind and sweet and loving, and the younger of the two. He also took a back seat to his older counterpart, Woody. As the first born of the household, Woody was a bossy boy who felt that Archie was brought into the house as a toy for Woody to play with.

But there was little laughing on this day, because Mrs. Flout had only one steak bone left from last night's dinner. She knew Archie would like a special treat and Woody, well, he just wouldn't survive on mere dog food alone.

"Oh dear," Mrs. Flout sung in her high-pitched voice, "With only one bone, I may just have to make you two little boys share." So, Francine Flout turned away from the kitchen counter to get one of her big, carving knives. "This one ought to do," she said proudly, and turned back with a knife so big and so long, it would put some butchers to shame.

"Oh no!" Mrs. Flout sputtered, with her eyes big and bulging and all turned about, "Where in the world; who in the world; I mean, what on earth has happened to the bone?"

There was only one little guy who knew, and that was Woody. Being the more aggressive of the two, and Mrs. Flout's shadow, Woody was either at her side or lurking nearby. He watched her every move and seemed to know exactly what she was going to do and when. Woody knew well that if he didn't go for that bone at that second, he wouldn't get what he thought was his fair share. He might even be forced to share.

You must realize that Woody was almost human. If it weren't for his bark, his tail and some of his hygiene habits, you might think he was Mrs. Flout's natural born son. He followed his mom to the kitchen, the bedroom and even to the bathroom. Why, when Mrs. Flout would draw herself an evening bath, Woody would sit atop the towels, keeping them warm until she was done. To Mrs.

Flout, Woody was every bit as good as a good son could be. After all, he always loved being with her, comforted her when she was sad and yipped and yelped when he wanted her attention. His big black eyes, surrounded by his mane of cream-colored curls, would stare right through her.

It's not that Mrs. Flout liked Woody any better than Archie. After all, Mrs. Flout rescued Archie from a mean, loner of a man who lived with hundreds of dogs and gave very little care. She figured Archie was not only neglected, but also as a sweet and shy little pup, never forced his way in with the other dogs to get his fair share. He had a great life with Mrs. Flout; good food, nice, long walks down country roads and plenty of love. Yet, Archie stayed to himself. He spent a good deal of the time under Mrs. Flout's favorite green armchair, where it was comfy and cozy and safe.

"Oh well," Mrs. Flout figured," Those two will have to work it out. I must go to the market and run my errands before the day slips away." So, she took off her apron, slipped on her flowered dress and ran some blush across her cheeks. "Good to go," Mrs. Flout exclaimed. "Now you boys behave and I'll be back soon."

It couldn't have been more than fifteen minutes later when Woody licked around the corners of his wet, black mouth and let out a large burp. Sitting right next to him was that steak bone — cleaned so well, there wasn't a trace of meat left. Woody carried it down to the basement, and dropped it into the corner, behind some old books for safekeeping. A bone is a prized possession to a dog; even a dog like Woody. Special care must be taken to keep it in eye's sight, but not so clearly as to call attention to it for others. You never know, Mrs. Flout might think he was done with it and throw it out. Even worse, Archie might spot it and take it as his own. No, this was serious business. A steak bone this good was meant to be saved, if only for a few more hours and a few more licks.

When Mrs. Flout returned, the two fluff balls ran to the door, tails wagging and eyes fixed on the doorknob. 'Mom' was back and it was time for the usual nighttime ritual. The little boys sat at Mrs. Flout's feet during dinner and on the couch while she watched her favorite nighttime television show.

"Time for bed," Mrs. Flout's high-pitched voice echoed through the house. In a flash, the two boys fell quickly in line; Woody first, then Archie. They followed

their mom up the stairs and into the beautiful room with the big, French doors. That was the special place for the night. They could rest their paws, throw up their ears and not have to worry about passing cars or children on bicycles or other dogs walking by. No, this was their place of peace, where they curled up with Francine Flout, let out a happy sigh as another day passed into night.

'Cock-a-doodle-do,' the rooster crowed from across the road. Flecks of sunlight streamed in through the lace curtains on the tall bedroom windows as morning came calling. Sometimes the light made designs on the bedspread and Woody and Archie tried to grab them, as if they were objects that landed in their bed. The furry little fluff balls had funny little morning routines. Woody stretched his legs far out in front and even further out in back, like an athlete stretching out before a big game. Archie covered his dark face with both paws, rubbing top to bottom, over and over again, as if to shake the dust out of his eyes. A couple of yawns and they were ready to start the day. You might guess where Woody's first stop was going to be.

Woody stretched out his paws, wiped the sleep from his eyes, jumped down off the bed and headed to the basement. Proudly, he trotted over to the corner, looked behind the stack of books where he had most carefully placed the bone and let out a howl that sounded quite a bit like a coyote. The bone was gone! How could this be? Did Mrs. Flout become a more careful housecleaner?

Did she find the bone and throw it away? She never looks in this corner with all of the cobwebs. Something was just not right.

While Woody looked everywhere, from corner to dusty corner, Archie sat nearby, watching him. Archie was so sweet and innocent, yet he had a look on his deep, black face that was unfamiliar. He almost looked like he was smiling. Did he know where the bone was? If he did, he didn't dare let it be known. His gaze was broken as Mrs. Flout called them to come eat.

Usually, they both came running, but not on this morning. Woody was hot on the trail of the missing bone and didn't even hear Mrs. Flout call him. Archie waltzed in, glad to see Francine Flout with not just one, but two juicy steaks bones lying on the kitchen counter.

"I felt so bad that my posse had to share one bone yesterday," said Mrs. Flout, "So I stopped at the butcher on the way home and picked up two more." Mrs. Flout placed one bone in each dog dish, and called Woody to come eat.

"Woody, oh Woody," Francine Flout called, "Where can my little guy be? This is so unlike him to be late for a meal." While Mrs. Flout began her own search for Woody, Archie carefully dragged one bone, and then the second, and placed them underneath his favorite chair. It was the last seen of those new bones that day.

That night, Woody looked exhausted from his day-long search. His head hung low, ears scraping the floor. His eyes tilted downward, he had a look on his face that you could only describe as a serious loss. Nothing like this had ever happened before. He always knew where he placed important things like bones, and where to find them. He was tired out. Before Mrs. Flout even called, he dragged his limp, little body up the stairs and headed for bed.

Woody jumped up onto the bed and took his regular position. But, something was different. He smelled something peculiar, something you would never find in Mrs. Flout's bed, something like food. He scrunched up his nose, raised his eyes and much to his surprise, there it was. He found the bone on Mrs. Flout's bed! But that wasn't all. He pushed one of the fluffy pillows aside and better yet, he found another bone — still  full of juicy red meat.

Woody looked around and saw Archie looking up at him. And at that moment, Woody knew that Archie had found his bone, which he wasn't all that happy about. Now Archie knew the best secret hiding place in the house too, making it not a secret anymore. But, why didn't he finish all the bones? Why was this one still meaty and juicy? Why didn't Archie just eat that one too?

At that moment, Archie let out a big burp and turned to smile at Woody. He was happy. He had found Woody's bone and given it a lick. He had eaten a new bone that 'Mom' was kind enough to buy, and still serve one to Woody in his special resting place. When Mrs. Flout walked in, she was tempted to yell at the little guys. They broke her rules and brought snacks into the bed. But she realized that something special was going on here.

"You two little guys are the best at sharing," Mrs. Flout said, as she turned off the light, "Wait till you see what treats I have for you tomorrow."

# Who Let the Dogs Out?

Mrs. Flout wiggled in her favorite green chair as she turned on the evening news. Of course her curly, canine companion — Woody wiggled along too. Archie was curled up at Mrs. Flout's terry cloth slippers, since Woody didn't like other dogs on the furniture.

"Oh, my little Frenchmen," Mrs. Flout cooed to them. "Let's see what on earth has happened in the world today."

Woody would never really understand Archie, just like so many pampered Poodles, Bichons and Pomeranians. You see Archie had not spent his whole life under the loving care of Mrs. Flout. He lived the first four years of his life in a crowded kennel, with lots of other dogs barking and fighting and stealing each other's food. It was only when Mrs. Flout rescued him and brought him home, did he come to know the wonderful life, comfy blankets and good food he was now enjoying.

"Oh dear," sang Mrs. Flout, as she watched the news reporter, "I cannot believe it - no, not again!" Now Woody was smart enough to know something was wrong, but not quite sure what it was. He bore down deeply into Francine Flout's apron and stared deeply into her big, blue eyes trying to catch her attention, But Mrs. Flout seemed too distracted. In fact, she let out an abrupt shout to end the evening, "Come on my little boys," she ordered, "We're going to bed."

Usually both fluffballs followed right behind their mom's feet. But Archie was nowhere in sight.

Mrs. Flout called out, "Archie, where are you? It's time for bed." This was most unusual, since Archie was so obedient. Francine and Woody checked every room downstairs. There was no sign of him in the kitchen, which of course, is a dog's favorite room. There was no sign of him under the green chair or in the study. There wasn't even any sign of Archie outside, where he usually made a bush stop before going to bed.

As they made it to the top of the stairs, Mrs. Flout could see one black ear dangling from the quilted bedspread.

"I guess Archie was in a hurry tonight," Mrs. Flout said to Woody, "He looks like a perfect, sleeping angel."

Bedtime was one of the most wonderful times of the day for the Little Frenchmen. There were no phones ringing, no mail arriving, no doorbells, no outdoor birds to feed. Nightime was a time to cuddle up next to Mom, let out a sigh, put up their paws and feel perfectly content with the world — but not this night. This night was different.

As soon as Mrs. Flout let out the first deep snort, which sent the pillow cases waving like a flag in the wind, Archie darted off the bed and headed downstairs. Woody opened one sleepy eye, following Archie's every move as long as he could without daring to move from his very comfortable blanket. But the snap of the dog door echoed through the quiet house, loud enough to make Woody curious enough to go downstairs and see just what Archie was up to.

But Archie was long gone. Woody pushed his way out through the dog door and sniffed and searched the backyard from top to bottom — no Archie. So he followed the fresh paw prints left in the wet ground to a loose board in the fence — so loose it flipped open when Woody nudged it a bit with his cold nose.

Woody just had to find Archie. First of all, how dare he just leave the house like that? After all, if there was any dog who would be taking a trip, it would most certainly be Woody. Secondly, why didn't Archie let on that he was on a mission? Didn't he trust Woody? And finally, Mrs. Flout would be terribly worried about Archie if he wasn't lying paws up in the bed come morning. Woody must follow the trail until he got to the bottom of things.

It was dark, it was cold and Woody walked for blocks, past some pretty odd characters. There were Cheshire cats lurking in garbage cans, a scruffy looking Terrier barking up a storm in one backyard and even a few very quick mice, running for cover under bushes.

"I can't believe the things I have to do," thought Woody, "It's not always easy being top dog."

Suddenly, Woody heard something strange. He heard barks and howls and dogs scratching. He looked up and sure enough, there was Archie, heading into a big red brick building. On the door, the sign only had five letters. It read ASPCA.

"What on earth is Archie up to?" Woody wondered, "I know I can't read, but I do know that I have seen the big, white truck with those letters on it, and almost always, I see dogs who don't have homes or families. This must be where they are taken." Woody believed he was a bit smarter than Archie, and certainly more aware. So, he looked around, took a deep breath and entered the building.

Woody was shocked. No stuffed chairs, no comfy beds and so many dogs just waiting to find a mom like Mrs. Flout. But where was Archie and why on earth did he come here? Before Woody could even begin to find it out, two Beagles came running down the hall towards him, then two Huskies, then three Terriers, a chubby Bulldog and a red Poodle. Behind the Poodle was no other than Archie, looking proud as punch and acting like a Sheepdog herding his flock. Woody gave him a stare — one like a mother gives her misbehaved child, but Archie marched on past Woody, giving him a smile as he continued on his mission. Totally shocked, Woody followed behind Archie, nudging him and jumping on him — just wanting to know what Archie thought he was doing. But Archie continued to herd the dogs from behind, past the Cheshire cats in the alley, the barking dogs, the scuffling mice — back to Mrs. Flout's backyard.

Woody was furious. "Just what do you think you are doing bringing all these dogs into Mrs. Flout's yard — our yard?" Woody wanted to know. But Archie just rounded the group up,  got them settled down for the night and headed back through the dog door, up the stairs and back onto the comfortable bed, where he once again dangled his ear off the side.

By this time, streams of light shone through the lace curtain, projecting their pretty designs on the bed. Mrs. Flout snorted one final time, rolled over and opened one eye. As usual Woody and Archie were in their favorite positions.

"Good morning, little men," Mrs. Flout sang out. "I just had a wonderful dream and you two gentlemen are going to be in for one big surprise."

Little did Mrs. Flout know that as soon as she got up, dressed and went downstairs to the kitchen, she was the one who was in for a surprise. A dozen or so big, small, cute, smelly, black, tan and even red dogs were camping out in her backyard. Loud barking made Mrs.

Flout rise from her bed, before she could shake off the sleepiness and fumble for her glasses.

"What on earth is going on here?" she asked, as she talked into the air. Woody and Archie beat it downstairs. They really didn't want to be around if Mrs. Flout got angry, and they wanted to calm down their new friends and figure out just how they were going to feed them all.

But Mrs. Flout was too quick on this morning. She cut Woody and Archie off at the entrance to the kitchen, before they could get to the backyard door.

"I don't know how or why or what in the world is going on here," Mrs. Flout sang in a flustered voice, "But I have a feeling that somehow, someway, you two little fluffballs are involved."

Both Woody and Archie, scrunched down into the floor and placed their heads upon Mrs. Flout's slippers; Woody on the left and Archie on the right. Just as they flashed that wide-eyed, loving look into Mrs. Flout's eyes, the phone rang.

"Hello. yes, I just awoke and found about a dozen in my yard," said Mrs. Flout. Four furry ears shot up as Woody and Archie listened carefully to what was being said.

"Oh they did," continued Mrs. Flout, "Well, I had a feeling that something was going on, but I had no idea. I'll look forward to seeing you in about an hour. Goodbye."

Mrs. Flout walked outside, and as always, every single dog came running to her, wagging their tails.

"Oh, you sweet things," she said, "It's been a strange night, but I have a feeling that this is your lucky day." Woody and Archie stood nearby, listening, not knowing what Mrs. Flout was going to do, and Woody still didn't really understand what was happening, but he knew that he was involved.

Ding-dong. The doorbell rang and it was Mrs. Flout's friend from the farm down the road. Woody and Archie watched as they chatted and hugged each other. The lady rounded up all the dogs and led them into a very large, red pickup truck, slammed the door and drove away.

Now Archie got extremely nervous. He ran to and from the door, jumping and barking, as though he was very upset.

"Oh Archie!" Mrs. Flout sang, "You are an unbelievable little Frenchman." Woody's ears perked up, since as far as he was concerned, the only unbelievable dog in this house was Woody. "You did a very kind and brave thing last night Archie. When I saw that kennel on the news last night, with all of those poor homeless dogs, I remember how you came to live here with us. I know why you had to go there last night and help those dogs find good homes. I'm very proud of you," Mrs. Flout went on, as she rubbed Archie's head and gave him a hug and kiss.

"I'm proud of you too, Woody, for going after Archie. It shows me just how proud you are to be a brother. Finally, you know how to share and play and get along with your brother." Woody was feeling mighty proud, listening to all the great things Mrs. Flout had to say about him. He stuck out his chest, lifted up his ears and believed that all was well, as he kept his proper place in the family — even if Mrs. Flout did have a few of her facts wrong.

"Since you have been such a good brother Woody , and you are such a sweetheart, Archie, you didn't even know that you made my dream come true." As the two Frenchmen looked at each other in a confused way, Mrs. Flout pulled out something from the dining room door behind her. They couldn't believe their eyes as she was holding a little red poodle:

"Guess what, my sweet little boys?" Mrs. Flout exclaimed, "Now that you have learned to get along so well, meet your new sister. Her name is Daisy. I just couldn't send her to the farm down the road. I had to keep her  now that there's more space in our hearts and in our family. Aren't you both thrilled?"

Woody took one look at Archie, thinking "Oh, brother!  Now look what you've done!"

**Now that you have read the adventures, track your favorite characters, stories and events from _The Adventures of the Poodle Posse._**

Which story do you like best? _____

_____

Why?_____

_____

Who is your favorite character?_____

Why?_____

_____

What color is Woody?_____

What color is Archie?_____

What is Mrs. Flout's first name?_____

What surprises you in the stories?_____

_____

_____

What makes you laugh in the stories?_____

_____

_____

What do you think will happen now that Daisy becomes a

member of the posse? _____

_____

_____

Would you like to let the author and/or illustrator know what
you think? They would like to hear from *posse* fans at
chrysasmith@verizon.net or www.wellbredbook.net.

## Happy tails to you!

**Feeling gratitude and not expressing it
is like wrapping a present and not giving it.**
—William Arthur Ward

*For partnership in book design, production and promotion —*
*Pat Achilles*

*For reviews, research, informed suggestion
and general helpfulness —*
*Karen Beem, Janine Daniels, Courtney Dietzel,
Devon Dietzel, Kasey Dietzel, Ruth Fields,
Linda Hastie, Jill Manning, Gail Richardson,
Dolores Rock, Claire Svendsen, Karen Wallace*

*For general inspiration —*
*Kathy Carey, Ruth Carlson, Jay Folkes, Jay Johnson,
Amy Murphy, Dorothy Parchinsky,
Bob Sandewicz, Mark Smith, Dane Smith, Cleta Szoke,
all my poodles (past and present)*